THE TALE OF THREE TREES

RETOLD BY

ANGELA ELWELL HUNT

The Tale of
Three Trees

ILLUSTRATIONS BY

Tim Jonke

LION
Children's Books

Text copyright © 1989 Angela Elwell Hunt
Illustrations copyright © 1989 Tim Jonke

Designed by Gary Gnidovic

Published by
Lion Publishing plc
Sandy Lane West, Oxford, England
www.lion-publishing.co.uk
ISBN 0 7459 2262 7

First edition 1989
First paperback edition 1992
10 9 8 7

A catalogue record for this book is available
from the British Library

Printed and bound in Malta

For generations the tale of three trees has been handed down from parents to children, retold in churches at Christmas and Easter; and even set to music and sung. As is often true of folktales, its originator is unknown. To this person, I am deeply grateful.

ANGELA ELWELL HUNT

Once upon a mountaintop, three little trees stood and dreamed of what they wanted to become when they grew up.

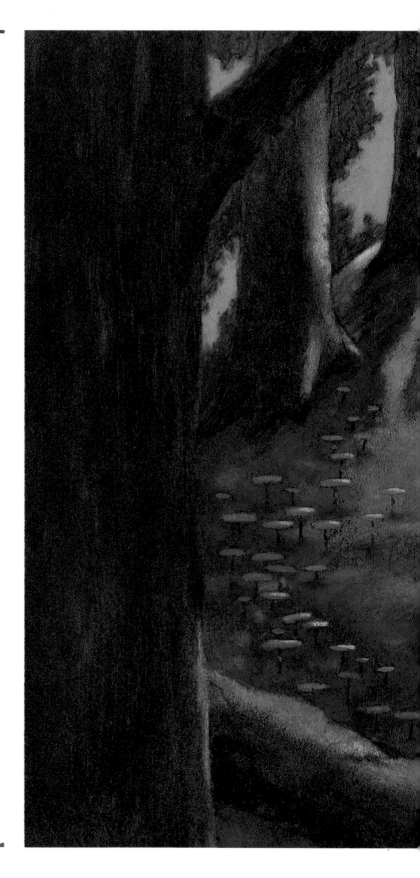

The first little tree looked up at the stars twinkling like diamonds above him. "I want to hold treasure," he said. "I want to be covered with gold and filled with precious stones. I will be the most beautiful treasure chest in the world!"

The second little tree looked out at the small stream trickling by on its way to the ocean. "I want to be a strong sailing ship," he said. "I want to travel mighty waters and carry powerful kings. I will be the strongest ship in the world!"

The third little tree looked down into the valley below where busy men and busy women worked in a busy town. "I don't want to leave this mountaintop at all," she said. "I want to grow so tall that when people stop to look at me they will raise their eyes to heaven and think of God. I will be the tallest tree in the world!"

Years passed. The rains came, the sun shone, and the little trees grew tall.

One day three woodcutters climbed the mountain.

The first woodcutter looked at the first tree and said, "This tree is beautiful. It is perfect for me." With a swoop of his shining axe, the first tree fell.

"Now I shall be made into a beautiful chest," thought the first tree. "I shall hold wonderful treasure."

The second woodcutter looked at the second tree and said, "This tree is strong. It is perfect for me." With a swoop of his shining axe, the second tree fell.

"Now I shall sail mighty waters," thought the second tree. "I shall be a strong ship fit for kings!"

The third tree felt her heart sink when the last woodcutter looked her way. She stood straight and tall and pointed bravely to heaven.

But the woodcutter never even looked up. "Any kind of tree will do for me," he muttered. With a swoop of his shining axe, the third tree fell.

The first tree rejoiced when the woodcutter brought him to a carpenter's shop, but the busy carpenter was not thinking about treasure chests. Instead his work-worn hands fashioned the tree into a feed box for animals.

The once-beautiful tree was not covered with gold or filled with treasure. He was coated with sawdust and filled with hay for hungry farm animals.

The second tree smiled when the woodcutter took him to a shipyard, but no mighty sailing ships were being made that day. Instead the once-strong tree was hammered and sawed into a simple fishing boat.

Too small and too weak to sail an ocean or even a river, he was taken to a little lake. Every day he brought in loads of dead, smelly fish.

The third tree was confused when the woodcutter cut her into strong beams and left her in a lumberyard.

"What happened?" the once-tall tree wondered. "All I ever wanted to do was stay on the mountaintop and point to God."

Many, many days and nights passed. The three trees nearly forgot their dreams.

But one night golden starlight poured over the first tree as a young woman placed her newborn baby in the feed box.

"I wish I could make a cradle for him," her husband whispered.

The mother squeezed his hand and smiled as the starlight shone on the smooth and sturdy wood. "This manger is beautiful," she said.

And suddenly the first tree knew he was holding the greatest treasure in the world.

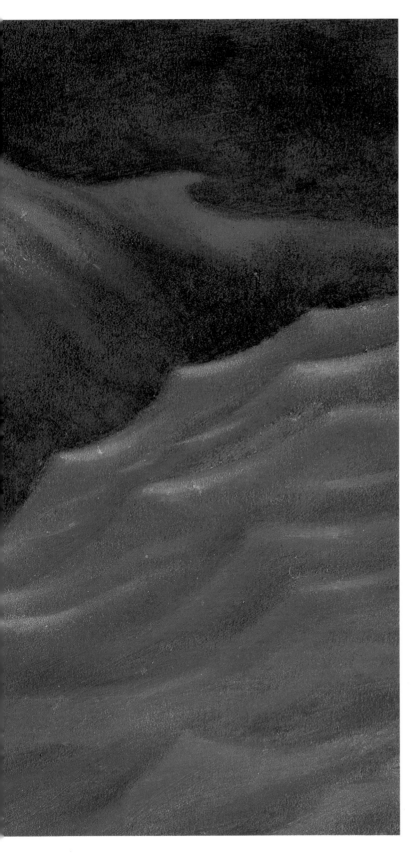

One evening a tired traveller and his friends crowded into the old fishing boat. The traveller fell asleep as the second tree quietly sailed out into the lake.

Soon a thundering and thrashing storm arose. The little tree shuddered. He knew he did not have the strength to carry so many passengers safely through the wind and rain.

The tired man awakened. He stood up, stretched out his hand, and said, "Peace." The storm stopped as quickly as it had begun.

And suddenly the second tree knew he was carrying the King of heaven and earth.

One Friday morning, the third tree was startled when her beams were yanked from the forgotten woodpile. She flinched as she was carried through an angry, jeering crowd. She shuddered when soldiers nailed a man's hands to her.

She felt ugly and harsh and cruel.

But on Sunday morning, when the sun rose and the earth trembled with joy beneath her, the third tree knew that God's love had changed everything.

It had made the first tree beautiful.

It had made the second tree strong.

And every time people thought of the third tree, they would think of God.

That was better than being
the tallest tree in the world.

Other picture storybooks in paperback from Lion Publishing

The Donkey's Day Out Ann Pilling

The Frightful Food Feud Brian Sibley

Giant-killer John Ryan

Jonah: A Whale of a Tale John Ryan

The Mouse and the Egg William Mayne

The Very Hungry Lions John Ryan

The Very Worried Sparrow Meryl Doney